This book belongs to:

Stuart Trotter

Big Bully Hippo

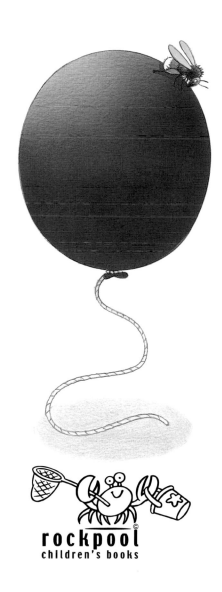

rockpool
children's books

For: Vicki, Lily, Edward and Tilly

Rockpool Children's Books
15 North Street
Marton
Warwickshire
CV23 9RJ

First published in Great Britain by Rockpool Children's Books Ltd. 2006
Text and Illustrations copyright © Stuart Trotter 2006
Stuart Trotter has asserted the moral rights
to be identified as the author and illustrator of this book.

ISBN 0-9553022-1-8
ISBN 978-0-9553022-1-3

Printed in China

Hippo looked out
of his window and said,
"What a lovely day for a walk."

Hippo splashed his way
through the water.

"Out of my way," he said rudely.

"What a big bully Hippo," said Duck.

"What a big bully Hippo," said the Fish.

Big Bully Hippo hadn't gone far when...

"Give me a ride,"
snapped
Big Bully Hippo.

"Say please,"
said Crocodile.

"Give me a drink,"
roared
Big Bully Hippo.

"Say please,"
said Lion.

"Give me a balloon,"
shouted
Big Bully Hippo.

"Say please," said
mummy Baboon.

"Give me a kick
of that ball."
boomed
Big Bully Hippo.

"I wouldn't kick
that if I were you,"
said Meerkat.

Too late!

"Buzzzzz,"
buzzed the bees.
They were very
angry.

"Get the bees off me!"
pawed Big Bully Hippo.

"Say please,"
said Elephant.

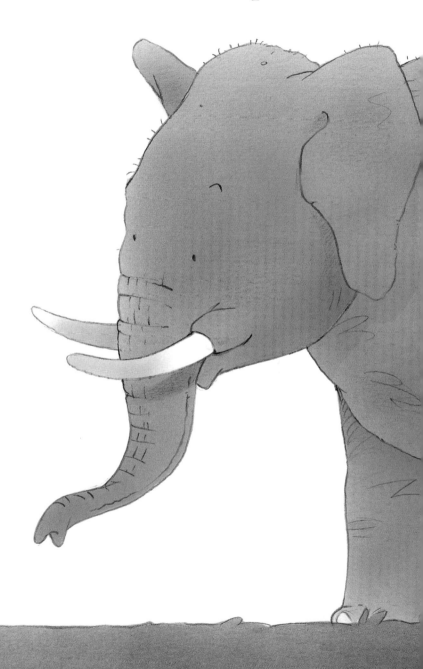

"Please!"

Elephant took
a big breath and...

blew the bees
away.

So Big Bully Hippo had said, "Please."
And he had said, "Thank you."

And

"Good morning."

a perfectly polite Hippo.